The Royal Nappy

NICHOLAS ALLAN

RED FOX

Some other books by Nicholas Allan:

Cinderella's Bum
Father Christmas Needs a Wee!
The Giant's Loo Roll
Heaven
Jesus' Christmas Party
Picasso's Trousers
The Queen's Knickers
Where Willy Went

THE ROYAL NAPPY
A RED FOX BOOK 978 1 782 95025 7

Published in Great Britain by Red Fox,
an imprint of Random House Children's Publishers UK
A Random House Group Company

This edition published 2013

1 3 5 7 9 10 8 6 4 2

Red Fox Books are published by Random House Children's Publishers UK,
61–63 Uxbridge Road, London W5 5SA

www.randomhousechildrens.co.uk
www.randomhouse.co.uk

Addresses for companies within The Random House Group Limited can be found at: www.randomhouse.co.uk/offices.htm

THE RANDOM HOUSE GROUP Limited Reg. No. 954009

Printed and bound in Italy

The Random House Group Limited supports The Forest Stewardship Council (FSC®), the leading
international forest-certification organisation. Our books carrying the FSC label are printed on FSC®-certified paper.
FSC is the only forest-certification scheme supported by the leading environmental organisations, including Greenpeace.
Our paper procurement policy can be found at www.randomhouse.co.uk/environment

MIX
Paper from
responsible sources
FSC
www.fsc.org
FSC® C013123

The Duke and Duchess look after the Baby Royal . . .

. . . but Nanny helps out.

Nanny tidies the Royal Nursery and prepares the Royal Pram,

but most of all sorts out . . .

. . . the Royal Nappy Cabinet.

Nanny has always looked after the Royal Nappies:

in the time
of the knights,

in the 19th century,

NAPPY
BAG

NAPPY
CASE

and even during the
First World War.

And Nanny, of course, knows the Royal Nappy-changing Song . . .

The Royal Nappy-changing Song was first sung to
King Henry VIII when he was a baby.

Henry loved to eat, especially meat pies,
so the song was sung a lot.

THE ROYAL
NAPPY-CHANGING SONG *

Oh dear, oh dear,
Oh what a to-do!
Our Royal Prince
Has had a great poo!
But here is a nappy
All fresh, white and new!
So HAPPY is Baby
With a Royal coo-COOO!

* Sung to the tune of *Greensleeves.*

Today's Nanny needs more nappies than ever before . . .

and she must keep track of them all in
the Royal Nappy Chronicles.

Everything runs smoothly because the Royal Nappies are printed at the Royal Mint, where the Queen prints all the money.

But one day they got mixed up. It caused . . .

There is a nappy for every occasion.

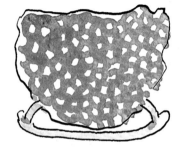

WINTER HOLIDAYS

ROYAL BABY
RUN
(Babies and
Royalty only)

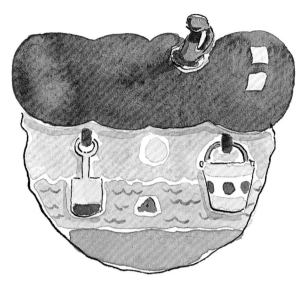

SUMMER HOLIDAYS

EASTER HOLIDAYS

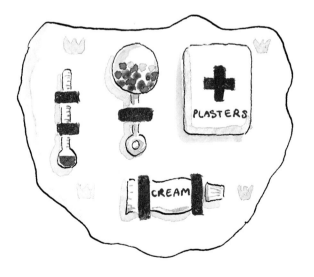

WHEN FEELING POORLY

FOR LISTENING TO LULLABIES

There are many flag nappies as the Duke and Duchess entertain lots of foreign visitors.

GERMANY

UNITED STATES OF AMERICA

CANADA

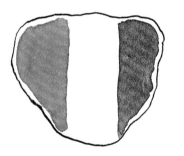

FRANCE

SOLOMON ISLANDS

MAURITIUS

BORA BORA

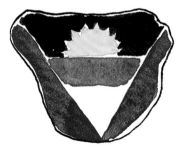

ANTIGUA

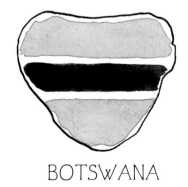

BOTSWANA

If the French Prime Minister comes to tea, then Baby wears the
French Flag Nappy, and if the President of China comes,
then Baby wears the Chinese Flag Nappy.

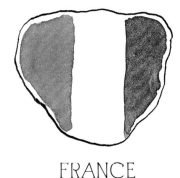

FRANCE

CHINA

If both visit at the same time, then it is helpful
if the Royal Nappy needs to be changed.

But I wonder what would happen if, one day,
Baby had a great Babies' Party at the Palace,

and **all** the nappies ran out!

And just then . . .

... the President
of the United States
was arriving in
Air Force One ...

. . . and Nanny couldn't get any more in time!

What would happen?

All would be revealed!

But if **I** was there with my baby sister,
then everything would be all right,

as Mummy **always** has a spare nappy ready for the other mummies.

In fact, today I've decided I will send
something special to Baby.

So I think the Duke and the Duchess
will be getting a little surprise in the post.